AF278906

Narcissistic Bee Bursted "ITS" Balloon

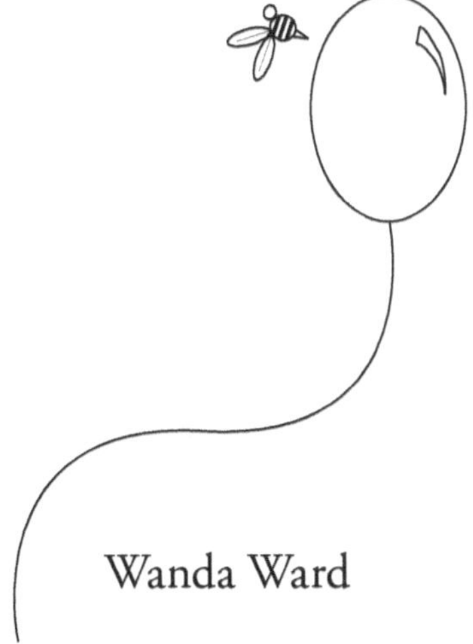

Wanda Ward

AuthorHouse™
1663 Liberty Drive, Suite 200
Bloomington, IN 47403
www.authorhouse.com
Phone: 1-800-839-8640

First published by AuthorHouse   6/11/2008

ISBN: 978-1-4343-6474-6 (sc)

Library of Congress Control Number: 2008900510

Printed in the United States of America
Bloomington, Indiana

This book is printed on acid-free paper.

Dedicating this to Candace, Sylvia and Sarah

The little world of childhood with its familiar surroundings is a model of the greater world. The more intensively the family has stamped its character upon the child, the more it will tend to feel and see its earlier miniature world again in the bigger world of adult life. Naturally, this is not a conscious, intellectual process.

C.J. JUNG

Narcissistic Bee
Bursted "ITS" Balloon

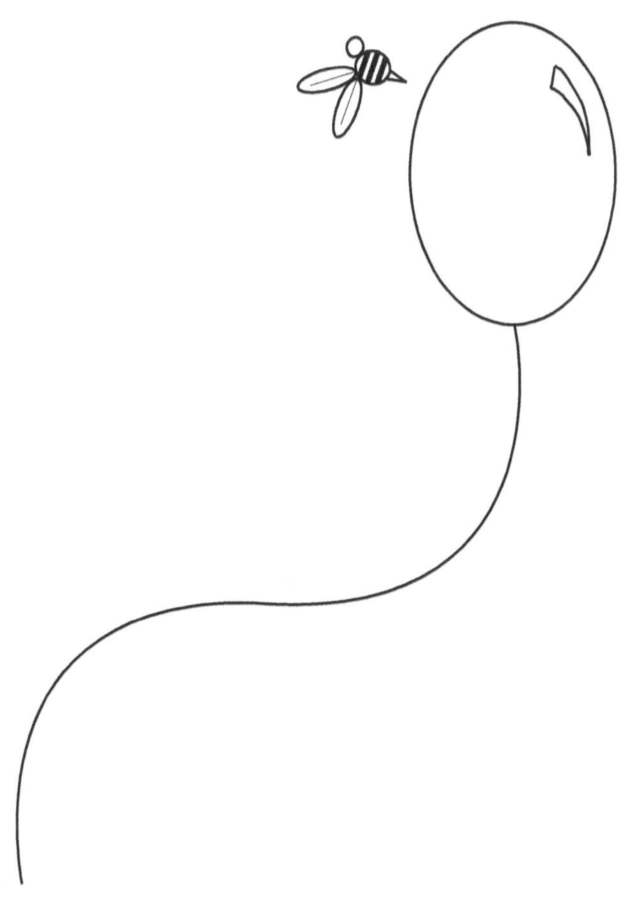

Narcisstic Queenly Arlene used her abusive tactics to burst "ITS" air balloon. That left hardly any air to breathe or even to survive on. This emotional condition has spanned my whole entire life.

ABUSIVE:

* constantly corrected "IT"
* put it down for doing things differently from hers
* used jokes or critical remarks to ridicule
* corrected "IT" publicly
* thinks her ideals and beliefs are gospel
* believes she is inately superior
* justifies her hurtful actions because she was supposed
    to be that way
* disregarded the feelings of "IT"
* she wanted severe emotional punishment for "IT"

When a child is treated emotionally badly by her mother and an older narcisstic sister from babyhood on, this instills into the child's young mind that it is the way he or she will look forward to accepting and being treated by the rest of the world. And if the child is scared and shy because of the emotional trauma heaped upon the poor defenseless mind, then he will be receiving more abuse by the outer world. People are ready to apply more abuse onto a "whipped" dog, whether they mean to or not, or probably laughing at the "poor little thing".

Arlene's most venemous adage was 'WANDA FERN COON SMITH, I'D BE ASHAMED OF MYSELF". Coon was mother's maiden name and it was an insult. If for some reason, it added to mother's pleasure. When this was accomplished, Arlene would twist her narcisstic head around and give me a " I PUT YOU DOWN" ugly grimace. Then her narcisstic ego grew mightily1

Mother was very elated to see that occured.

When people looked at while I was displaying the effects of sister"s Narcisstic ego, they would feel sorry for me and ask "What is the matter with you"? I certainly could not tell them. This always brought back my post traumatic distress!

WHAT IS POST-TRAUMATIC STRESS DISORDER?

Posttraumatic stress disorder (PTSD) is an anxiety disorder that can occur following exposure to a traumatic event that caused intense fear, helplessness, or horror. PTSD can result from personally experienced traumas (e.g., rape, war, natural disasters, abuse, serious accidents, captivity) or from the witnessing or learning of a violent or tragic event. While it is common to experience a brief state of anxiety or depression after such occurrences, those with PTSD continually re-experience the traumatic event; avoid individuals, thoughts, or situations associated with the event; and exhibit symptoms of increased arousal. Those diagnosed with PTSD experience these symptoms for longer than one month and are unable to function as they did before the event. PTSD usually appears within three months of the traumatic experience, but in some circumstances can surface months or even years later.

HOW COMMON IS PTSD?

Studies suggest that anywhere between two percent and nine percent of the population h as had a bout with PTSD. However, the likelihood of developing the disorder is increased by exposure to multiple traumas and traumas experienced early in life, especially if they are prolonged or repeated. Increased incidences of the disorder have also been found among inner-city youths and those recently immigrated from troubled countries. Additionally, women seem to get PTSD more frequently than men.

Veterans are perhaps the community most associated with PTSD, or what was once referred to as "shell shock" or "battle fatigue." The Anxiety Disorders Association of America notes that an estimated 15 percent to 30 percent of the 3.5 million men and women who served in Vietnam have suffered from PTSD.

What are the symptoms of PTSD?

Although the symptoms for individuals with PTSD can vary considerably, they generally fall into three categories:

- *Re-experience*—Individuals with PTSD often experience recurrent and intrusive recollections of and/or nightmares about the stressful event. Some may experience flashbacks, hallucinations, or other vivid feelings of the event happening again. Others experience great psychological or physiological distress when certain things (objects, situations, etc.) remind them of the event.

- *Avoidance*—Many with PTSD will persistently avoid things that remind them of the traumatic event. This can result in avoiding everything from thoughts, feelings, or conversations associated with the incident to activities, places, or people that cause them to recall the event. In others there may be a general lack of responsiveness signaled by an inability to recall aspects of the trauma,

Being born into a family with a Narcisstic older sister was the hellish environment that molded my life. Being reared under these conditions, I was trained to let Arlene always be the leader or decision maker. If I said or did anything on my own or acted first, I was put down by her and Mother, usually out in public. I learned to keep my mouth shut!!! Mothers usually reprimand their children by using their whole names to get their attention. She never did, but she let Arlene do the damage "Wanda Fern Coon Smith, I'd be ashamed of myself"!! Then they'd both laugh, and agree and confer together, while I died inside. These things were burned into my mind. I could not stand up for myself, because Arlene would become very vicious. Not only was I emotionally abused, but I was also physically abused by having to do all the hard work Mother needed done. When Mother detailed the chores she wanted done, Arlene would yell out from somewhere she was hiding "Make IT do it, she doesn't have anything else to do"!! I always had to do it, or we would not have any drinking water carried in for fixing supper. Our water had to be carried from a well about a quarter of a mile from our house. I knew it would have to be me, so I would grab the buckets and get out of there so I would not have to listen to Arlene's yelling and griping about me. These were examples of the many incidents which shaped and scarred my emotional life. My childhood, married life, employment, and as a mother to children I brought into the world has failed and been a total wreck. I have been told now, that I had developed alters to assuage my mind. I needed several alters to help me get through into my old age. But I was so badly scarred that I am now not being understood by doctors I see or have seen, nurses who condemn me, and I have been barred by the two hospitals who have also given me "NOT TO BE ADMITTED'111

Being labeled as an "IT" kid and being treated as a worthless piece of JUNK was very dehumanizing and debasing to a very young child, especially as it was continued all through my grade school years by my mother and older sister, along with Mother's twelve brothers and sisters. The first time I ever heard my name was when my father took me to school for the first time and gave the teacher my real whole name. It took a long time to get used to using it and then to be going home and be "IT" again. If I protested, my mother and sister would make a big joke of it and shame me for protesting. I learned to keep my mouth shut or go off somewhere and cry. Father would intercede for me when he was around, but he was usually out working, so I had to take care of myself. Father's inherited Amish tenets and my mother's wild Irish traits did not produce a stable and comfortable family home life. Three sons were born first and neither lived. Then came my sister, born four years before me. Mother never wanted any other children but her "beautiful" daughter and then I came along and spoiled everything for her. Her attitude towards me and the family environment caused sister to develop her Narcisstic personality. Mother condoned it encouraged and abetted this personality trait to continue to develop in spite of my father's protests. "IT" was the one who fed her ego by enduring their constant physical and intensified abuse emotionally. This constant abuse led me to going into another state of mind, developing "alters". They became my friends. Of course, I was not aware of them then.

Troubled started for me on a beautiful October day. No, actually it started before that as a fetus. I only weighed about three pounds at birth and was not expected to live. Mother was very obese and short. Due to the cramped conditions, I was also very short and one of my hips had developed about a half inch shorter than the other one. Mother and sister always considered me to be defective, thus labeling me the "IT" thing. I had to learn to cope with that for many years.

MY earliest recollection of being "alive" was at the very early age of three or four weeks. Mother was holding me and was yelling at my father in another room. All of a sudden she threw me down on the hard floor. I landed hard on my back. She leaned over and grabbed me and slammed me back down on the hard floor. This time my head hit hard. My father came in and rescued me. I don't remember anything else but my head hurting and my father saying "thank God, she's all right". I tried to smile at him. This would have been her "accident". She had a lot of those, somehow I was involved in many of them. When I was in my crawling stage there was another "accident". AS I was crawling around on the kitchen floor, I came to an open door. I crawled into the pantry. There was a THING of interest in there and I put my hand on it. The thing snapped. It snapped on my fingers and almost cut them off. I never had anything hurt so badly in my life, either then or later. It was a trapper's steel trap. Father rescued me again and I know he was berating her for leaving the door open. All she ever said was "I did not know that the IT would go in there". She was the oldest in her family and had to help care for all of her younger siblings She never tried to ease my pain. Evidently all of her compassion had expired before I came along. In all the years I have lived and suffered mishaps, those two accidents were the worst physical pain I"ve ever endured.

Her twelve brothers and sisters also contributed to my "IT" status. They teased and harrassed me when I was a baby lying in my crib. They pinched, poked, punched me and pulled and twisted my nose until the tears came. Father would stop them if he was around, but Mother always laughed and joined in their fun. When they were finished with their physical abuse they would heap guilt and shame on me by "poor little thing, Cat got your tongue, bashful little thing, look at it trying to hide, shamey shamey, and better learn to talk". Mother would scold me some more after they had gone. I was only a baby and did not know the words to say to make them stop. On other occasions when other people were around and talked nicely to me she would pinch me or admonish me in some other covert way not to answer them. Then when they were gone, she would berate me again for not talking to them. This was a double whammy for me! I would go off by myself to cry and try to reason the WHY. I decided not to talk at all unless I had to and hide from danger if I could. This led to my "loner" personality taking over. My lonerism alter comforted me. I was considered acting funny, but never laughed at school, because I was always at the head of the class or close to it. They respected me for that. All except my sister who was always running home from school to beat me and tell Mother what "IT" did at school today. Whether good or bad, they would laugh and shame or describe to me what I should have done. Then sister would throw up her head and give me a hateful look and I could see her Narcisstic ego grow another notch or two every time she received praise from Mother by taking me down and could watch me cry. My loner alter kept me from joining into many activities at school or other public places. If we played cards or croquet or did any other activity at home and I won, then she would throw a tantrum and she never entered into that activity again. Mother always consoled her and it seemed that I was at fault. Father would tell her to make Arlene mind and give her a good spanking. But "Arlene is my oldest daughter and I could never give her a spanking". I never got many spankings either because when I saw her come running at me, I would crawl under the bed or run away and hide. If I could not get away fast enough, then she would grab my hair and give it a pull and shake. This was usually for not talking. I learned to stay out of the house or go off into the woods to climb trees. Sometimes I would go to the fields to watch my father working in the harvest. Sometimes he would take me with him out where he was working when he saw her angry rages toward me.

Being reared in this atmosphere of treatment by my sister and mother created an umbrella of social inadquacy, fear, shame, and guilty feelings which have hung over me all of my life and shaped my behavior. As I acted accordingly, other people, not understanding why, have added to my emotional damage whether they meant to or not. As I was behaving differently, no one could know, and neither did I know that I had developed alters to protect myself.

When I was twelve years old my father died of pneumonia. Now I was really alone. We moved to town and I finished my eighth grade. I really tried hard to make a few friends. Sister did not seem to be able ro acquire any, so she followed me and my few friends around for awhile until they dropped me because of her Narcisstic personality. She always had to be the leader. So I was a loner again all through high school and I liked it. I had to survive this thing. Teachers were appreciative of a quiet and intelligent student and doing my homework was good at first. Then sister decided that her ego needed inflating again. It was me again, because who else was there and with Father gone, she could be as cruel as she could make herself. As I was struggling with Algebra, she saw her golden opportunity. She'd grab the textbook and sit on it until I caved in. Well that wasn't cruel enough, then she'd tear my up finished assignments or throw them into the fire. If I tried to get back the book or my homework, she would grab my wrists and hang on in a tight vise like grip and hold on for dear life. I would try to get away to no avail, and Mother was watching and laughing, telling me that I had to learn to get along with sister. As I struggled to get away my sister would apprise me of her beauty, how ugly I was, had no friends and no man would ever go out with an ugly thing like me. When her ego became sated she would make me promise not to do anything to her and to "behave myself". Then I'd have to do homework all over and massage my sore wrists. Then came that hateful look of triumph which she always gave me when her ego became satisfied. Every time this happened, I would die inside, but I never did hit my sister. She always won and would twist her ugly head in the most despisable way that she had. This went on all through my high school years. When she graduated a couple of years before me, then she was gone to her job for a lot of the time, so I did have peace until she would come home on vacation. Then she really poured it on. Mother was so proud of her working and she joined in with her. They ordered me around and treated me like a servant. I was ordered to do all the work which they decided was too much for them. I had to comply because that was the way they had my life programmed and I saw no way to avoid it. At this time, I really contemplated suicide. But during that summer, I made friends with a girl my age who was having problems at home, too. and we would get together and talk about our woes and what we could do about it. One day, we decided both together, that we would not take it any more. So we decided to run away. Since the next day was Sunday and we had a date with a couple of boys we had been seeing, we set it up. I packed a small bag with a few necessities and sneaked out of the house. No one said anything to us. I was ignored unless they wanted some job done. Nancy and I had been going around with these boys before for a while, and they had asked us to marry them. When they saw our bags , I believe they thought we had taken them up on their offers. I felt no guilt as we drove off, only a big relief. When we heard the boys talking about going over into Kansas where anyone could get married any time without delay ,we panicked, and started giving each other baffled looks as we drove along. By the time we reached Kansas City, we were ready to jump out of the car and run.

It was around midnight when we got to Kansas City and the only place that seemed to be open was a bus stop and cafe. We stop ed there for a rest and a bite to eat. Nancy nudged me to get my bad and "we'll be back". We took off to look for the rest room, instead we went out a side door where a big bus was just loading. We did not have tickets but were allowed to get on and purchase them at some other bus stop along the way. The sign on the bus said California! We got on as the bus pulled out. What a relief that the boys did not catch us! We rode all through the night until we came to this small town on the KS and CO border. A new cafe and bus stop had just opened up there. We stopped and bought our tickets and ate. While we were eating, a throng of the harvesters came in ready to eat, there were no waitresses or other help. The manager came over and offered us the job. We did and it was fun, we had a cabin of our own to live in. We worked for a couple of weeks, and then Nancy sort of fell for this harvester who came in to eat. He and his buddy wanted us to go with them to the harvest festival in Wichita. In the meantime, I had sent a post card home to say we were OK. I wish that I had not, because when we got to the festival we were picked up by police and spent the night in a lock up. The next morning our home town sheriff showed up and drove us home. I was dropped off at my house. No greeting, sister seemed shocked, and Mother greeted me as usual with hair puling and now even fists. She never cared to ask where I had been or if I was all right. Her rages went on like this for three or four days, until one night I had the guts to slip out and meet Nancy to see what had happened with her. It was pretty late when I got back to the house, but she had waited up for me. She was coming at me really fast. I thought of my large school book on the table. I picked it up and told her "you'll never hit me again". She passed on by and went on to bed. No, she did not hit me again. She even began to show a little respect for me. I was still wary around her for quite a while.

She never did hit me or pull my hair again, but the emotional abuses continued by both of them. This time by making fun of my friends and running off any boys who came to call on me. I numbed myself and tried to go on with my life. After graduating from high school, I went on and enrolled in college, and there I met my husband. I got married at eighteen, and it was heaven to get away from the, but that dark emotional umbrella still hung over me which ruled my behavior. Twenty years and four children later, I found myself being divorced by a man who could not stand my behavior either. I did not think my behavior was all that bad! I decided to return to college to finish my teaching degree. Professors soon noticed my "behavior". Some were really rude to me, ordering me to go see some man. I guess he was a counselor, but we did not know about counseling back then, so I was afraid to go see him. It soon seemed that they were all coming down on me emotionally and lowering my grades, so I went to see the man. No answers, so I never went back. They finally let me graduate and I found a good teaching position in that area. About ten years later, I went to work on the Indian Reservations in the southwest. No one noticed or cared about how I acted there, in fact, I fit in well there. After about twenty years I retired and came back to the midwest. I was free to live my life as I pleased, even though that old dark cloud hung over me. Mother had been dead for a long time, and the sister, I never saw. She lived far away. I was a loner but I was almost satisfied with my life. Except for the arthritis which had begun to bother me. I made an appointment with a good doctor and went into his office for the first time. This doctor came into the room with a big smile on his face saying " Oh, have you got a beautiful sister"? It stunned me to think why this doctor would have any connection to my "beautiful sister". Trauma set in and I began to cry. He sent me to see a psychiatrist. PTSD. The psychiatrist did not recognize it as such, and he did nothing for me but give some pills which made me so dizzy, that I had to get rid of them fast. PTSD traumas were really resurfacing at odd times and I became quite concerned, for this had never happened before. I made an appointment to see a psychologist and unloaded on her. I could see that she did not understand at all. She diagnosed me as being depressed, and ordered me to go to another hospital and check myself in for shock theatment. I did not want to get electric shock. Then the whole MERCY HOSPITAL that she worked for came down on me emotionally, the same way that the college had, and I checked myself into another psychiatric facility, there the psychologists were more up to date with psychology. I discarded the tranquillizer that the other psychologist had prescribed for me. It was lethal, and I could have taken it and commited suicide or been rushed to that other hospital for the shock treatment.

My new psychologist made me bring in the tranquillizers and flush them down the toilet. She was very kind. She did not order me to get on my hands and crawl to the sister, the way the other psychologist had done. She diagnosed me as DID, or having alters. Thank the

Lord, and the psychologist, I know why people could not understand my behavior. Since seeing this very up to date psychologist, I have been feeling that the old emotional cloud is finally lifting. I, also wrote a very straightforward letter to the sister telling her what she was, and what she had helped Mother do to my life. I did not get an answer, as I knew her ego would not permit her to say she was sorry or anything else. I will not see her again!

Dissociative disorders are so-called because they are marked by a dissociation from or interruption of a person's fundamental aspects of waking consciousness (such as one's personal identity, one's personal history, etc.). Dissociative disorders come in many forms, the most famous of which is dissociative identity disorder (formerly known as multiple personality disorder). All of the dissociative disorders are thought to stem from trauma experienced by the individual with this disorder. The dissociative aspect is thought to be a coping mechanism – the person literally dissociates himself from a situation or experience too traumatic to integrate with his conscious self. Symptoms of these disorders, or even one or more of the disorders themselves, are also seen in a number of other mental illnesses, including post-traumatic stress disorder, panic disorder, and obsessive compulsive disorder.

Dissociative amnesia: This disorder is characterized by a blocking out of critical personal information, usually of a traumatic or stressful nature. Dissociative amnesia, unlike other types of amnesia, does not result from other medical trauma (e.g. a blow to the head). Dissociative amnesia has several subtypes:

- *Localized amnesia* is present in an individual who has no memory of specific events that took place, usually traumatic. The loss of memory is localized with a specific window of time. For example, a survivor of a car wreck who has no memory of the experience until two days later is experiencing localized amnesia.

- *Selective amnesia* happens when a person can recall only small parts of events that took place in a defined period of time. For example, an abuse victim may recall only some parts of the series of events around the abuse.

- *Generalized amnesia* is diagnosed when a person's amnesia encompasses his or her entire life.

- *Systematized amnesia* is characterized by a loss of memory for a specific category of information. A person with this disorder might, for example, be missing all memories about one specific family member.

Dissociative fugue is a rare disorder. An individual with dissociative fugue suddenly and unexpectedly takes physical leave of his or her surroundings and sets off on a journey of some kind. These journeys can last hours, or even several days or months. Individuals experiencing a dissociative fugue have traveled over thousands of miles. An individual in a fugue state is unaware of or confused about his identity, and in some cases will assume a new identity (although this is the exceptoin).

Dissociative identity disorder (DID), which has been known as multiple personality disorder, is the most famous of the dissociative disorders. An individual suffering from DID has more than one distinct identity or personality state that surfaces in the individual on a recurring basis This disorder is also marked by differences in memory which vary with the individual's "alters," or other personalities. For more information on this, request the NAMI factsheet on dissociative identity disorder.

Being out in the field sin bright summer sunlight surrounded by nature and all its wonders, I was feeling wonderfully alive. Arlene, my sister who was four years older than me, was helping me pick blackberries for a pie. They were black, sweet and juicy and our mother would make us a pie for supper. She was a very good cook and we always had everything we could want to eat on the table. The cookie jar was always full, too. Looking out over yonder fields we could watch our father working the harvest. Mother, Father, sister and

I were a close knit family living off the land during the '30s. Since I was the baby of the family and very very small for my age, the family had lovingly dubbed me the "IT". I knew my real name Fern, but but didn"t mind being called "IT". There were no close neighbors and very few children our ages so we forged our own family community with our own rules set by our parents. Reflecting on our family"s history, we knew that our father was the son of Amish parents, who had left their home in Germany, to start a new life in America. They left the Amish church, but brought their Amish tenets along. That became the structure of our family. He met and married my mother, a red-headed, fun loving Irish woman, and when sister and I came along, we became a happy family unit.

Life was peaceful living with an older sister who played with me and taught me a lot of the things she had learned at school. We had never had a disagreement or fight, like we had watched our cousins do when they visited at our house.

Sister indicated that the bucket was full, so we started back to the house, stopping by the barn lot on the way back to pet our baby mule "Janet". She was perfect and one of the very few red ones around. That color was in demand, and father could sell it for a high price to someone who had a red one and wanted to have a matched team. When he sold her, we would never be riding in the buggy and driving her to the store. That was a treat because Mother always took me in the buggy with her when she went to the store for something. The store people there were generous with their suckers and balloons. I always had some to take home to sister.

Since Mother had been a teacher, she was teaching sister and me at home. When I was four years old, I could do everything that first graders could do, so Mother sent me to school. It was easy work, but I was afraid of the two older girls there. When the bell rang for bathroom break time, they would lock the smaller girls out so we could not get in. Then when school started we could not leave the room to go use the bathroom. As a result I had an accident in the school room. I was sent home for the rest of the year. The next year, I did both grades together and went on to the third grade.

My father's Amish relatives were gentle, loving people. Grandfather Smith was my favorite. When he died and we went to his funeral, I became obsessed with death. Seeing his body being lowered into the grave gave me ideas. I wanted to know what would happen to his body, the minister said he was going up to heaven. When we got home, I cut up my little rubber doll and stuffed the pieces into an empty kitchen matchbox. Then I took it out to the flower bed and buried it deep. I waited quite a while and then went out to dig it up, or to see if it was there but I never did find it. I dug so many holes in the yard, that I finally had to stop looking. I supposed that there was a heaven for Grandfather and my doll. My life was like a dream world sometimes, when I'd spend hours in the woods alone, building playhouses or climbing trees and dreaming of the future. It went on like this until I was 12 years old, when our father who was bothered with asthma, developed pneumonia and died. We moved to a small berg with a high school. I as a Freshman. My sunny, friendly personality seemed to be disappearing. My father was the one who encouraged that to develop, and now he was gone. I had no one to be fun with. I felt very much alone. So I became obsessed with lessons and schoolwork, there was no time for friends and certainly no boys! I had become a loner and did not care. I was vsery relieved when I finally graduated and went on to enrol in this small college. There the students, faculty and their activities were cohesive. It was like living in a commune. I abhorred this "sticky" business and acted accordingly. I arrived to class very early to get myself assigned to a seat. It was always the first seat in the first row. Then there was only one person on my left to contend with. This was my "honor seat" and it was always mine. No one seemed to mind or contest it. After graduating from this place, I went on to a larger college to work on a master's degree.

This college, being larger, was more open and not so "sticky". Students and faculty were not fraternizing with each other. Or at least it was not so visible.

I was always aware of being a loner in crowds or out anywhere. My mind always assessed the situations and drew its own conclusions. With ESP, I was always nearly one hundred per cent correct. People around me in crowds or fellow students in the classrooms seemed to be in limbo. Their voices would rise in conversation, sometimes arguing moot problems, things of little or no importance. My mind would become numbed to their conversations, it was like listening to a swarm of bees. How I wanted to leave their presence, but if I was in the classroom, I would make myself endure it. I did not want to be rude. As soon as the class was over, I was the first one out the door, very relieved.

In crowds, if anyone came too close to me, I would assess the situation. If they came too close to me, I would move, or I would figure out a way to make them leave my space. Usually it would work like hitting them with my purse or nudging them with "Excuse me, I was afraid you were going to step on my sore toe." That usually did work. I always did assess the space thing before going into a crowd, though.

At my age, now retired, I really am at rest with this lonerism. I do not see anyone unless I want to, or have to. I have my little chihuahua, Charlie Brown to keep me on my toes and to converse with. Other people have wanted me to volunteer. I hate it when they try to force me to do that, because I am retired from their crowd now. I would gain no benefits from mixing in with nonloners again. I get my benefits when I am alone, and my mind does its own thing. I keep it active by reading, listening to musis, or just sitting and mediating. During mediation with myself, I can work out solutions for my problems. If I needed help I could always find it at the library, or get it from a person of authority, not from a mob of nonloners who probably could not come to an agreement on anything.

Loners are born, not made! We have trouble making and keeping friends. I have had only three true and lasting friends outside of my husband. Two were high school classmates, and the other was a psychology student. When these friendships were dissolved I was emotionally scarred, and resolved not to entertain any more relationships of that nature and to that degree. I will rely on my own resources to bring me peace of mind.

Listening to my old familiar and favorite music evokes some of the more pleasurable experiences I have experienced during my lifetime. My mind becomes numbed to my problems and enviroment. I experience unmeasurable pleasure and my mind is at ease. I can cope with my life for a while longer. My Doctor tells me that when I do this, I am hyptonizing myself.

I understand that I had met and married a person just like myself, a loner. We loved each other but not madly. I loved being married to Don, and tried to bring back my old friendly, happy and fun loving person that I had been before my father died. I tried very hard because I wanted my husband and children to follow my example. But due to housing problems and Don't job changes we were never able to establish ties to any community. We were loners and this was not good for the children, especially in school.

When our oldest son was born, Arlene started showing up at our house bearing expensive presents for him, as well as for the others, but they were more expensive for Jay. Don did not want her around, because he said that she was mean to me, and that she was buying our oldest son's affection. Jay became obsessed with her and adopted her Narcisstic personality.

His father and I tried desperately to stem its growth, but as he went through his teen years he looked upon his father and me as nothings. He ignored us and as soon as he graduated from high school, he packed his belongings and went to live with her. She tried to adopt him, but that never happened for some reason or other. During all this time Arlene was being married and divorced and still showing up at our house flaunting her queenly attitude. And still being mean to me.

Our other son was born with a slight handicap, which Don blamed me for. I could sense that he was now unhappy and wanted to be free. Still two other beautiful daughters were born and when the youngest was two years old, he decided that he wanted a divorce. It was done, and he was so happy to be free that he forgot his children, no visits, no XMAS or anything, no letters and he never once tried to see or communicate with them in any way. He married an older woman he had met at a bar, someone to drink and smoke with. He died soon afterwards. I was really relieved when he died, because the children were adults now and he was trying to interject himself back into their lives. He was whining and begging them for money and favors. This was the very things which he had withheld from them all through their growing years.

The next twenty five years of my life was spent teaching special education students in the public schools and on the Indian Reservations in the Southwest. Actually that time period is nearly blotted from my mind. I have to try really hard to recall any events occuring during this era. It was a peaceful time, no Arlene to boss me. So I actually began to feel human and develop a little confidence within myself. Arlene's shadow was still there. At the age of seventy, I was diagnosed as being affected by PTSD. During therapy, my alters were uncovered. They were pointed out to me by a caring and very perceptive psychologist, who helped me to deal with and put them "together". It was that dissociative identity disorder which had disrupted my whole life. Now I finally know what was wrong with me, why people could not understand me or like the way I acted. It was caused by physical abuse and severe emotional trauma during my childhood from infancy on.

It was so severe that it clouded, threatned and disrupted my whole life. At my age it is difficult if not impossible to reorganize and regain any good part of my past life. I started by writing to my sister who had played a major part of my past life which was destroyed. And also, by labeling me the "IT THING". I told her what she had done to me and how I wish she could have been different. I never got an answer, I know that I never will.

All of my life, being around a bossy, queenly older sister was not conducive to my having developed any degree of confidence of self esteem. She under cut almost everything that I ever said or did. If I got a smile or a pat on the back from anyone or anything she came across to me with what she had gotten much better. I saw no need to argue with her and swallowed my hurt feelings. Mother usually was in gleeful agreement with her. As I grew older and was more on my own, I began to take things, usually when I was being cheated or being rude to my mainly store clerks. I could not stand up to those kinds no more than I could stand up to Arlene. I knew that what I was doing was wrong but I could not help myself. This went on until I was seeing this psychologist for PTSD. She helped me to curb this bad behavior, and in the meantime my other mean alter was coming forward. This one wrote a cruel and nasty letter to Arlene. This one was a very lengthly one and I described in detail what all she had done to her "IT". This one was sent by registered mail, so

I knew she'd get it. She did. I was not able to tell her those things to her face, even when I got older. She was very vicious when crossed face to face. There are also other people in my life who have abused ne, mainly, the psychology department and the whole hospital staff of the Mercy Hospital which I had been going to for the last five years. They were having fun with me. The thing which they were all in was a big 'set up fiasco'. It was very cruel because the entire hospital was brought into it by the psychologist I had been seeing for PTSD. She never recognized PTSD. I was emotionally 'stung' by remarks and abusive treatment when I had to be in in touch with any of them. One new nurse lied on me and got me expelled from my doctor's office. I had been seeing him for almost five years, and this hurt. Various other people, the social worker, nurses and Dr.s along with the psycholigist would call me at my home and order me to check myself into the other hospital for shock treatment.

Not Mercy Hospital!! I was slmost emotionally broken down, but I pulled myself together and went to another psychiatric facility. There I unloaded my problem about what they had done to me. I guess my mean alter came to help me. I was using all the vile, nasty language that I could think of. I really do not remember all the words describing what they had tried to do to me. This very helpful lady helped me when she could and listened to all of my griping. One day when I was describing one of them in vivid, nasty words, I looked over and saw her sitting quietly and listening. This shameful feeling came over me all of a sudden and I thought ' Oh1 I like this lady, and why am I sitting here and using all this foul language in front of her?' I apologized several times and cut it off there. I haven't used vile words again and really can't remember any of what I had been saying. The whole Mercy Hospital and staff should be brought to realize what they have done to me. The nurse and psychologist should be put non probation for the harm that they caused me, so they will not try it on some other poor defensless woman.

I wanted to bring to justice the whole entire Mercy Staff for what they had done to me, and so they would not be trying it on some other poor old person. I had a notebook full of nearly everything they had said or did to me, either in their offices or when they called me in my home to berate me. No lawyer would not even listen to me because it was not physically observable!! It was both physical and emotionally hell for me. Near the end, my doctor prescribed medication for me to take. I did take one and if I had taken more I believe it would have killed me or sent me to that hospital, which was what they wanted to happen! I filed a complaint two times in a court of law describing what they had tried to do to me. This was laughed at. Mental Health is not acknowledged, recognizable even by lawyers and courts of law. Dissociative Identity Disordered people are created shaped and molded into iron cast molds that can not be changed without a lot of theraputic effort by professionals trained in that field. This molding and shaping has been done to the child before the ages of four or five years of age. Emotionally traumatic episodes at these early ages causes the child's mind to learn to think and react in different ways to get past the trauma and hurt. Their mind even blots out the traumas or creates in their young minds other ways to deal with and assuage their damaged egos.

Arlene, my Narcisstic sister, was very stern and strict. She could or would not accept any of my feelings or reactions, She would not accept anything but what was up to her standards. She tried to inflict her self-rightous attitudes on to me. That and with Mother laughing and rewarding her behavior was my downfall. I suffered traumatic emotional injury and carried these feelings and emotions all of my life. I wanted so badly to be a normal person but could not. I now realize that I will not be free until I die.

Now in my retirement years, I have been turning to God and religion wondering why I could not seek out when I was still a child, or why I had been born into that situation.

There is one precept engraved into my mind: that we are each put on earth to fulfill a purpose. Searching long and hard , I can not find mine and certainally will not during my declining years, CONCLUSION: I was put here to build up, aid and abet and also endure my sister's Narcisstic ego. If this is so, her ego surely did bloom. I should receive triple A's for my sisterly attitude. I never once hit her or say mean and nasty things to her. I always gave into her wishes and demands more than once. I helped her out financially a lot of times. As during one of her divorces, a plot of farm land was auctioneered off to settle the divorce. I quickly bid a dollar for it and was able to purchase it for a measley dollar. No one else had placed a bid. After the lawyer finished the paperwork, I singed the land back over to Arlene. She never said thanks to me. She knew what I was there for. I was proud to do it for her, sisters are supposed to love and help each other!!!

As my father lay dying, he told mother that he was going to die and that she needed to get tough with Arlene, make her mind, and stop the abuse she was heaping onto her little sister. She always came up with the same answer "Oh! I can't do that to Arlene, she is my oldest one"

Things began to get mightily worse from then on.

I would have appreciated dying at that time along with my Father, the only person who cared anything about me. I would not have to recall my traumatic life.

If Arlene dies before I do, I have promised myself that I'll not attend her funeral, because I know that she would rise up in the casket and deliver that old familiar insulting adage to me in front of the audience: "WANDA FERN COON SMITH, I'D BE ASHAMED OF MYSELF!" (Coon was Mother's maiden name.)

Will there ever be justice for the Civil Rights and wrongs which projected onto me by the Mercy Hospital and the other hospital, through which I was denied access to the ER, Urgent Care along with their doctor's offices. The big FIASCO was orchestrated by a Mercy psychologist, and a former doctor and also a Mercy psychiatrist. They hurt me, they diagnosed me and ordered me to go to that other hospital to get shock treatment. Their social worker called me at my own home and ordered me to do just THAT. This was a misdiagnoses. No other doctor has diagnosed me as THAT.

I have a whole notebook full of their actions along with phone recordings of some of the messages which they relayed to me on my phone in my own home. It was a years worth of harassment and I still can not be accepted by most of their doctor's offices or ER and urgent care facilities. I thank the LORD that my health is holding out.

I was told by both facilities that I would be turned away.

If the Civil Rights will not accept what they have to me, then there will be no justice for some one who has become so badly emotionally scarred as I have been. Actually I have presented this to Attorneys and Court of Law. They have even laughed at me along with Mercy and the other hospital alone with some of rheir Doctors.

As a Mother, Grandmother or as a friend to anyone I have never revealed any of the incidents and hurts which causes the pain and emotional sufferings that I have gone through all of my life. It was laid on to me by Arlene; " It was your fault." This is the messages I received from her and Mother!!

I did not want my children to be burdened by knowing anything about it. The only thing they detected was the way I acted or was forced to act by Arlene. She was a powerful slave driver in that area.

After his graduation from high school, Jay became so ashamed of my behavior, that he left home to go claim Arlene as his " Mother and Grandmother" for his two girls. I have been out of his life for more than twenty years. No calls, letters and no visits to maybe see my granddaughters.

Lois, my oldest daughter, divorced me with a mean and hateful letter as soon as she finished all of her schooling and became a Psychiatrist. She never described to me why she was doing what she did. We were really close before. I guess she became ashamed of her mother and wanted to begin another kind of life style. No calls or letters for more than twenty years or more.

Paul, my second son suffered brain injury at birth. He was not accepted in any way by Arlene. She treated him the same as me.

Ellen, my youngest daughter actually accepts the way I behave, or at least she has not divorced me yet. She is the mother of a beautiful daughter, my granddaughter. I see her occassionally because I do not want to inject myself into her life. I see that she may have a wonderful future. she does not want to be around someone who was controlled by a Narcisstic person. Some of that bad behavior could be absorbed by her. God bless her and protect her from what I was born into.